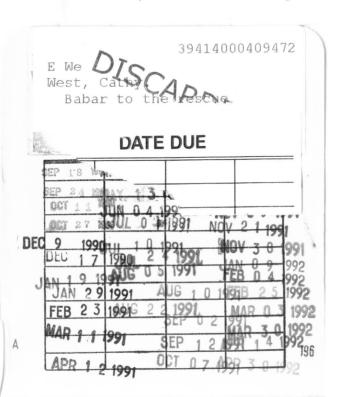

39414000409472

E We
West, Cathy
Babar to the rescue.

DISCARD

DATE DUE

SEP 18		
SEP 24	MAY 1 3	
OCT 11	JUN 0 4 199	
OCT 27	JUL 0 3 1991	NOV 2 1 1991
DEC 9 1990	1 0 1991	NOV 3 0 1991
DEC 1 7 1990	2 7 1991	0 9 1992
JAN 1 9 199	AUG 0 5 1991	FEB 0 4 1992
JAN 2 9 1991	AUG 1 0 1991	FEB 2 5 1992
FEB 2 3 1991	2 2 1991	MAR 0 3 1992
MAR 1 1 1991	SEP 0 2	MAR 3 0 1992
	SEP 1 2 1991	1 4 1992
APR 1 2 1991	OCT 0 7 1991	APR 3 0 1992

BABAR™
TO THE RESCUE
Based on BABAR—THE MOVIE

By Cathy West

Illustrated by Cathy Beylon

Random House 🏠 New York

Copyright © 1989 by Nelvana Ltd. All rights reserved under International and Pan-American Cop[...]
Inc., New York, and simultaneously in Canada by Random House of Canada Limited, Toronto. Bas[...]
and Raymond Jafelice. BABAR characters are trademarks of Laurent de Brunhoff. Produced und[...]
Library of Congress Cataloging-in-Publication Data:
West, Cathy. Babar to the rescue : based on Babar—the movie / by Cathy West ; illustrated b[...]
SUMMARY: After riding in the Victory Day parade, King Babar recounts the exciting story of ho[...]
ISBN: 0-394-84529-3 [I. Elephants—Fiction] I. Beylon, Cathy, ill. II. Babar—the movie. III. Ti[...]
Manufactured in the United States of America 1 2 3 4 5 6 7 8 9 10

903371

It was a very special day in the land of the elephants, called Victory Day. Everyone crowded along the street to watch the royal parade.

The children laughed at the clowns and squealed with delight as a huge elephant balloon bobbed across the sky.

The royal coach appeared. King Babar and Queen Celeste
waved to their loyal friends. Their children—Pom, Flora,
Alexander, and Isabelle—threw candies to the crowd.

At bedtime Babar's children were still far too excited
to sleep.

"Please tell us a story, Papa," begged tiny Isabelle.

"We want to hear the story of Victory Day!" cried
Alexander.

Babar gave in easily. He liked stories as much as the children did! "All right," he said, and the children shushed one another as they settled down to listen.

"The story begins years ago, when I was just a boy…"

It was young Babar's first day as king. It wasn't quite as exciting as he had dreamed it would be. Too much talk and paperwork! He tried to hide a yawn as his advisers discussed ideas for the new parade mascot.

Suddenly Babar's friend Celeste burst into the room. She had just come from far beyond the city's walls.

"You must send your army at once!" she begged breathlessly. "The rhinos are going to destroy my grandfather's village!"

Babar sent Celeste to tell the villagers that help was on the way. But old Cornelius said it would take *three days* to get the army ready!

"I can't wait that long to help Celeste!" thought Babar. So he convinced his cousin Arthur, who looked very much like Babar, to pretend to be the king.

Then Babar slipped out of the castle into the dark night.

But the jungle was a strange, dark place to an elephant raised in the city!

Finally, after hours of searching through the
dark night for the village, Babar saw a blazing light
up ahead.

"Oh, no!" cried Babar. "The village is on fire!"

The cruel rhino army was burning down the village and capturing the elephants to be their slaves!

"Celeste! Celeste! Where are you!" cried Babar. At last he found her. Poor Celeste! The rhinos were dragging her mother away.

But what could two small elephants possibly do to stop a huge rhino army? they wondered.

"We'll find a way!" Babar said as he and Celeste headed into the jungle.

They had to hurry if they wanted to follow the army's trail. Still, Babar took the time to rescue a little monkey from the jaws of a crocodile.

"You saved my life," said the monkey, whose name was
Zephir. "Now I owe you a favor in return—that's the law of
the jungle.

"We will meet again!" he added, waving as Babar and Celeste
continued their journey.

Finally Babar and Celeste came to the great fortress of the rhinos. They were able to sneak in by hiding in the back of a wagon—but were soon captured by rhino guards!

Babar spoke bravely to Rataxes, the leader of the rhinos:
"I am Babar the King, and I demand that you release all the
elephants!"

But Rataxes only laughed. "I am going to crush your puny
kingdom!" he shouted. "And no tiny elephant is going to
stop me!"

The guards locked Babar and Celeste in the dungeon.
"A fine king I am," Babar said sadly. "The rhinos are
going to destroy my kingdom—and there is nothing I
can do to stop them."

Suddenly Babar and Celeste heard a familiar chatter.
It was Zephir! He had sneaked past the guards to rescue
his friends.

Celeste ran to release her mother.
How good it was to be free again!

Celeste's mother stayed to help the other elephants escape. Babar, Celeste, and Zephir hurried into the jungle. Maybe they could still reach the castle in time to warn the elephants of Rataxes' plan.

But the mighty rhinos had already reached the castle! The three friends crept close to the camp so that they could hear the rhinos' plan.

"We attack at dawn!" Rataxes ordered his army.

Inside the castle everyone was arguing about what to do. "You must decide, Your Majesty!" Cornelius told Arthur, who was still pretending to be king. Poor Arthur didn't know what to do!

Babar ran into the room. He quickly explained to the bewildered Cornelius how he and Arthur had traded places.

"But there is no more time for talk— it is time for action," Babar said. "I have an idea, but we must hurry if we are to make it work."

Soon everyone was busy working in the early morning light.
Some sewed big gray flannel blankets together. Others blew up
balloons. The royal drummers lined up with their instruments.
Babar made sure that everyone had something to do.

Finally everything was ready. The young king bravely stepped outside the castle walls. "I am King Babar," he said. "I demand that you go away, or we will feed you to our giant elephant!"

Rataxes only laughed. "Your tricks do not fool us!" he shouted.

Suddenly the ground trembled with the sound of huge booming footsteps. A giant elephant rose fiercely above the castle walls!

The rhinos were terrified! They stumbled over one another as they ran away into the jungle. Rataxes shouted at them to come back, but no one was listening to him anymore.

Babar's idea had worked! The giant elephant was only made of balloons covered with gray flannel. The royal drums had made the big booming footsteps.

All the elephants cheered for Babar.

"You are going to make a fine king!" declared old Cornelius.

"And that is why we celebrate Victory Day each year," said King Babar as he gently tucked his children in.

And soon they were dreaming of their own great Victory Day adventures.